SOFIA MARTINEZ

The Marigold Mess

by Jacqueline Jules
illustrated by Kim Smith

PICTURE WINDOW BOOKS
a capstone imprint

Sofia Martinez is published by
Picture Window Books, a Capstone Imprint
1710 Roe Crest Drive
North Mankato, MN 56003
www.capstonepub.com

Library of Congress Cataloging-in-Publication Data
Jules, Jacqueline, 1956- author.
The marigold mess / by Jacqueline Jules ; illustrated by Kim Smith.
pages cm. -- (Sofia Martinez)

Summary: Instead of the usual dusting Sofia volunteers to wash the car — but when she leaves the hose on her mother's marigolds get flooded and she calls on her sisters to save the situation

ISBN 978-1-4795-5776-9 (library binding)
ISBN 978-1-4795-5780-6 (pbk.)
ISBN 978-1-4795-6208-4 (ebook)

1. Hispanic American children — Juvenile fiction. 2. Hispanic American families — Juvenile fiction. 3. Chores —Juvenile fiction. 4. Sisters — Juvenile fiction. [1. Hispanic Americans — Fiction. 2. Family life —Fiction. 3. Chores —Fiction. 4. Sisters — Fiction.] I. Smith, Kim, 1986- illustrator. II. Title.
PZ7.J92947Mar 2015 [E]—dc23
2014025328

Designer: Kay Fraser

Printed in the United States of America in Stevens Point, Wisconsin.
092014 008479WZS15

TABLE OF CONTENTS

CHAPTER 1

A New Chore

Sofia dragged the feather duster over the coffee table. It was Sofia's job to dust. Elena swept the floors. Luisa emptied the trash.

"Every Saturday morning it's the same thing," Sofia moaned. "Chores are so boring."

"I'm tired of dusting," Sofia told Papá. "Can I please have a different job today?"

"Why don't you wash the car instead? I'll dust," he said.

"¡Fantástico!" Sofia said.

Papá took Sofia outside and helped her fill a bucket with soap and water. He gave her a big yellow sponge.

"First scrub off the dirt. Then spray the car with the hose," he said.

"¡Perfecto!" Sofia said. "Spraying will be the best part!"

Papá pointed at the marigold garden next to the driveway.

"Be careful around the flowers," he said. "I planted those for Mamá."

"¡Claro!" Sofia promised. "I will be extra careful."

Sofia got busy right away. She dunked the sponge and scrubbed. Dunk and scrub. Dunk and scrub. Her cousin Hector ran over to help.

“Your car looks like it’s covered in whipped cream,” he said.

“Yo sé,” Sofia said as she giggled. “Maybe it’s time I sprayed a little.”

She went to get the hose while Hector picked up the sponge. When Sofia came back, Hector was leaning down, soaping the front wheel.

"¡Cuidado!" she grinned as she started spraying the hose at him.

As Hector jumped to get out of the way, he bumped the side mirror. “Ouch!”

Sofia dropped the hose. “Are you okay?”

Hector rubbed his arm. “I am, but the mirror isn’t.”

“Oh, no! You broke it!” she shouted.

CHAPTER 2

Trouble

Sofia and Hector ran to the house. Luisa and Elena heard all the noise and met them at the door.

"¡Ayúdanos!" Sofia cried.

"What did you do?" Elena asked.

"¡Rápido!" Sofia pulled on her sisters' arms.

When they got back to the car, there was even more trouble. A big stream of water was flowing across the driveway, right into Mamá's flower garden.

"Oh, no! I left the water running!" Sofia screamed.

"Mamá's marigolds!" Luisa said.

Sofia hurried to shut the water off. The yellow flowers looked like they were swimming.

Using her hands, Sofia pushed water out of the garden. Luisa, Elena, and Hector tried to help.

After a while, the garden wasn't flooded. But the flowers were still really droopy.

"We definitely need more dirt," Luisa said.

"Mamá keeps big bags for planting by the side of the house," Sofia said.

"¡Vámonos!" Elena said.

Together, they dragged the heavy bags back to the flower garden and ripped them open.

They spread dirt until every marigold stood up straight again.

"That looks a lot better," Sofia said as she wiped her dirty hands on her skirt.

"But we don't!" Hector said.

They stared at each other. Their faces, hands, and clothes were all covered in mud.

CHAPTER 3

A Muddy Mess

Just then, Papá came outside. "¿Qué pasa?" he asked.

"I dropped the hose and flooded the flowers," Sofia said.

"Oh, Sofia," he said.

"We also broke the mirror on the car," Sofia said, near tears.

Her heart thumped as Papá looked at the mirror.

"Lo siento," Sofia said quietly.

Papá simply pushed the folded mirror back into place and smiled.

"You fixed it!" Hector clapped.

Papá laughed. "The mirror was never broken. It was made to swing in and out."

"Thank goodness," Sofia said.

"Will the flowers be okay?' Luisa asked.

Papá checked. "Sí. You did a good job saving them."

"Gracias," Sofia held out her arms to hug Papá. He stepped back and grinned.

"I don't need to get dirty, too," he said.

Sofia looked at her muddy clothes, then over at Hector, Elena, and Luisa.

"We are so dirty," Elena said.

"We definitely need a bath!" Luisa said.

“Or a shower,” Sofia said as she turned on the faucet. Elena and Luisa squealed as Sofia pointed the sprayer at them.

“Move away from the garden,” she warned, smiling.

"Don't forget that the car needs a shower, too," Papá said.

"Sí, Papá," laughed Sofia. "And don't forget to dust!"

Spanish Glossary

ayúdanos — help us

claro — of course

cuidado — careful

fantástico — fantastic

gracias — thank you

lo siento — I'm sorry

mamá — mom

papá — dad

perfecto — perfect

qué pasa — what's wrong

rápido — quick

sí — yes

vámonos — let's go

yo sé — I know

Talk It Out

1. Nobody likes doing chores, but they are necessary. Why is it important to help with chores?

2. When trouble started, do you think Sofia should have told her dad right away? Why or why not?

3. Were you surprised about how Sofia's dad reacted to the situation? Why or why not?

Write It Down

1. Louisa, Elena, and Hector helped Sofia. Write about a time when you helped a friend.

2. Write a paragraph explaining what you would do if you were in Sofia's situation.

3. Pick your three favorite Spanish words or phrases from the story. Write three sentences using what you learned.

About the Author

Jacqueline Jules is the award-winning author of twenty-five children's books, including *No English* (2012 Forward National Literature Award), *Zapato Power: Freddie Ramos Takes Off* (2010 CYBILS Literary Award, Maryland Blue Crab Young Reader Honor Award, and ALSC Great Early Elementary Reads), and *Freddie Ramos Makes a Splash* (named on 2013 List of Best Children's Books of the Year by Bank Street College Committee).

When not reading, writing, or teaching, Jacqueline enjoys time with her family in Northern Virginia.

About the Illustrator

Kim Smith has worked in magazines, advertising, animation, and children's gaming. She studied illustration at the Alberta College of Art and Design in Calgary, Alberta.

Kim is the illustrator of the upcoming middle-grade mystery series *The Ghost and Max Monroe*, the picture book *Over the River and Through the Woods*, and the cover of the forthcoming middle-grade novel *How to Make a Million*. She resides in Calgary, Alberta.